Oscars Road Trip

By David Evans

Table of Contents

Chapter 1 10

Chapter 2 18

Chapter 3 47

Chapter 4 58

Oscar was fifty years old and lived in a cabin in Vermont.

The cottage had two bedrooms and one small bathroom.

It also had two medium-sized windows.

These windows were well insulated for the cold winters.

In his living room was a fireplace. However, he could only just fit two small logs in the fireplace.

Above the mantel is a trophy whitetail buck; it's a five-by-five buck.

He hunted this buck going back three years now.

Along with him on that hunt was his best friend Leone.

Leone is an architect and has made millions. Oscar has been to Leon's house many times.

He's forty years old and has a son named Larry. Larry is five years old. Larry is a good little boy. Oscar has a bad habit of drinking whiskey.

Oscar has known Leone ever since high school, he used to be a professional rock climber in his younger days.

Oscar has a younger brother, who is six years younger than him.

Oscar enjoys spending time with his younger brother as much as possible.

However, his younger brother lives an hour and a half away from him, in the small town, with a population of eight hundred people.

He gets along well with the town folk.

He drives a nineteen eighty-seven pickup truck. Over the years, he's kept it in good shape.

He has a dirt driveway, and it’s bumpy.

After it rains, his driveway gets deep ruts in it, and when he goes over them, the muddy water splashes up on the sides of his truck.

He's very meticulous about his vehicle.

He doesn’t like it when there are mud stains on his vehicle.

He has a plow for his truck that he keeps in his large shed.

He bought the plow new; he has had the plow for his vehicle for over four years and is beginning to get rusty.

He uses the plow hard every winter.

One year he left the plow outside in the elements, that contributed to the rust problem.

He has been on four road trips before, this year he wants to go on another one.

He likes to drive from the East Coast to the West Coast.

The four road trips had taken him all over the United States.

On the first road trip that he was on, he drove to Fort Worth, Texas, then moved to Washington D.C. he likes to check out the museums in Washington.

On the second road trip, he went from North Dakota to Florida.

The third time he went on a trip, he drove to Las Vegas and then drove to Canada.

By the fourth road trip, he was getting tired.

He would wait one year between every road trip that he went on.

Chapter 1:

On the fourth road trip, he went from California to Maine.

While driving to Maine, the truck's engine shut down on him, and smoke came up from the radiator.

Unfortunately, he wasn’t near a big city at the time.

He was two miles from the nearest town in Maine, he slammed his hands down on the steering wheel with anger and then put his head down.

After he was angry, he got out of his truck and opened the hood; there was no smoke coming out any longer from the radiator.

Along the way, the radiator must have run out of anti-freeze and burned up.

Then the unthinkable happened.

As he was looking at the engine, the fan belt came off.

He couldn't believe it and slammed the hood shut again and shook his head in anger.

He leaned on the hood of the truck and thought to himself, can things any worse than they are now?

He began to stare down the road.

As he was starring, a bull moose came walking out of the woods and onto the street fifty feet away from him.

The moose glanced over at him and crossed the road back into the woods.

He was Leary on what was going to come out of the woods next.

A car didn’t pass by him for going on ten minutes.

He thought, oh well, maybe my luck is going to change, I’ll be able to get out of here.

His truck was plenty far enough off of the road, and a white car came speeding past him.

He came so close to him that he jumped over the hood and was now standing at the truck's passenger door.

He thought, boy, that was a close call.

The car never stopped and kept on going on.

A few minutes later, a tractor-trailer that was hailing wood went speeding past him.

As the tractor-trailer was going past, a long log fell out of the truck's back and was rolling his way.

He ran as far back as he could from the log that was moving; he thought to himself, oh no, there goes my truck.

The log narrowly missed hitting his vehicle.

The log stopped rolling and was now in the middle of the road.

He thought to himself, now who's going to move that massive log out of here.

After that, he took out his cell phone to dial the towing company, but there was not enough signal to make a call.

As he was looking into his phone, he happened to think that the next vehicle that was going to come by was going to crash right into the log.

He was still on the shoulder of the road.

Knowing that an accident would happen at any moment, he decided to walk along a path that led into the forested area.

As he was walking the path, a few bugs began to buzz around his head.

He usually tolerates bugs pretty well, but this Day was different.

He didn't go far into the woods; he was now ten feet off of the road.

A car came down the road, and the driver slammed on the brakes as soon as he saw the log.

There was no way traffic could go past on either side of the street.

His phone still didn't get a good enough signal where he was standing.

The driver of the car got out and was a hothead.

He slammed his car door shut and began to walk over to the log.

However, he didn't see Oscar because he was in the wooded area.

The man was wearing a black suit with a blue tie.

He had a cup of coffee in his left hand.

Then in a fit of anger, he threw the cup of coffee down on the road right in front of him.

The man proceeded on towards the log and was cracking his knuckles.

Once he was right in front of the log, he bent down and tried to move it himself.

He tried with all of his might, and the log still wouldn't budge.

The man soon gave up after trying to move the log for ten minutes.

As the man turned around, a large black truck didn't stop in time and slammed into the back of the man's car.

With so much force that caused the vehicle to be pushed off the road.

The man didn't have time to act, and the truck plowed into him, throwing him up into the air.

The man's shoes went one way, and his body went another.

The crashed into the log; the log caused the driver to lose control.

The log and the truck were off the side of the road.

Oscar couldn't believe what he had just witnessed.

He felt so bad for what had happened.

He wondered if the man was still alive and if the driver of the truck perished.

So many thoughts ran through his head.

After all this, he happened to look over at his truck, and it was still there.

He couldn't believe it.

He ran over to where the man's body was lying.

He bent down and felt for a pulse.

There was no pulse, the mans both legs were all bloody, and his nose was broken.

He felt the guy's shoulders, and they were dislocated.

The man's fine suit was torn to pieces.

Oscar was upset about the man's deaths but realized no way to revive the man because he was too far gone.

Then Oscar stood up and ran over to the truck that was sixty yards away from him.

6

The car had hit a tree, and smoke was coming out of the hood.

The front of the truck was smashed in, and the bumper had fallen off.

The windshield had a big crack in the center of it.

The passenger side door was wedged in between another tree.

So, he couldn’t get into the truck that way.

He happened to look down and saw that the car was leaking oil.

He quickly ran around to the driver's side door.

The driver's head was leaning up against the steering wheel.

Blood was coming out of the gash on the man's forehead.

The seat belt was tightly against the man's chest.

To get the man loose from the seat belt.

He opened the driver's side door, and the guy's body was falling out of the truck.

So, Oscar grabbed hold of the man's shoulders and legs and slowly the man's body onto the ground.

Blood was coming out of the man's nose.

Oscar felt like he had to do something right away for the man.

The air was brisk, and Oscar knew that the man was going to get cold, so he took off his jacket and placed it over the man.

Oscar had a thick long sleeve shirt on, so he was going to be okay.

He quickly took out his cell phone, and this time his phone had enough signal to make a call.

His hands trembled as he dialed 911, the phone rang twice, and the operator picked up.

"911, what's your emergency?"

"I witnessed a serious car accident."

"When did the accident happen?"

"It happened ten minutes ago."

"Is the driver awake?"

"No," he's not Sir.

"How soon can you send out an ambulance, Sir?"

"We can send one out in five minutes."

“There was another innocent Sir “

"Okay, and what else happened?"

"A man was struck by the truck before it crashed."

"Is the man breathing?"

"No," he’s not.

"How long ago did he stop breathing?"

"Right after he was struck."

The truck was going at high speed when the man was struck; okay, thanks for telling me those details.

"What are you doing now?"

"I'm standing over the driver of the truck that crashed, Sir."

"Stay there until the ambulance gets there."

"Should I try to stop traffic, Sir?"

"No," don't do that; you will be at risk of getting hurt.

Just please be patient, the ambulance is on route and will be there shortly.

I hope that the driver survives Sir, he'll be okay once the ambulance gets there.

Oscar was breathing heavily while he was standing by the injured man.

He was getting tired of standing, so he leaned against the truck.

"Are you still there?"

"Yes," I am Sir.

Chapter 2

Wait just a little longer.

Okay, but my phone's battery is going down, Sir.

Don't worry about the battery in your cellphone Oscar, keep me on the phone.

Moments later, a woman went jogging by the accident.

She stopped for a moment and looked over at the scene.

She had a perturbed look on her face.

She had earphones in and was probably listening to something.

She continued to look at the scene for another few minutes and then went on jogging out of sight.

Oscar thought to himself that person must be out of their mind to jog out here.

That thought soon left him.

Then Oscar heard sirens in the distance.

"Hello Sir, yes?"

"I can hear the sirens of the ambulance."

"Should I hang up now, Sir?"

"Yes," you can

Thanks for letting us know of the accident Oscar, you're very welcome, Sir.

Then he hung up the phone and placed it back into his left side pants pocket.

Five minutes later, he could see the ambulance coming his way.

Oscar backed up from the injured man, allowing the EMTs to get the stretcher over by the wounded man.

One of the EMTs looked over at Oscar.

"Hello Sir, what's your name?"

"Oscar."

We appreciate you standing by the injured man. You're welcome, Sir.

While the other EMT's were too focused on their job to stop and say hello.

It didn’t take the EMT's long to get the stretcher loaded up into the back of the ambulance.

The driver was just about to get into the ambulance and looked back at Oscar.

"Excuse me, yes, Sir?"

"I almost forget to ask you if you wanted to ride in the ambulance?"

"I would, but I have to stay here with my broken-down truck, and besides that, I’m a stranger to the patient."

We have strangers who go with people that they don't know most of the time.

"Are you sure?"

"Yes," I'm sure.

Then I'll see you later, Oscar and the driver waved goodbye to one another.

After the ambulance left, the feeling of loneliness set in.

Oscar looked down and noticed that the EMT's had left his jacket lying in the street.

He heard the crash of thunder somewhere off in the distance.

He thought to himself, oh great; now it's going to rain on me while I'm stuck out here, and who knows, it could be a lightning storm.

He then decided to get back into his truck just in case it would start raining and pulled out his cell phone from his pocket.

He pressed the power button, it immediately turned on.

He remembered the phone number of the tow truck company, he quickly dialed the number and put the phone up to his right ear.

His phone rang twice before someone picked.

A woman answered the phone.

"Hello, Sir, what are you calling us about?"

"I'm broken down on the side of the road on a back road in Maine."

Unfortunately, the tow truck company is an hour away from you.

I don't like being called Sir all the time, Ma'am. My name is Oscar.

"How long will it take for a tow truck to come out here, Ma'am?"

"Exactly one hour."

"Are you inside of the vehicle?"

"Yes, I am, and why would you ask me that, Ma'am?"

"I just don't want you to get lost."

I would never abandon my vehicle Ma'am; some people leave their vehicles behind and walk down the road.

"Have you seen any wildlife out their?"

"Yes," my I have, and how does that tie into our conversation, Ma'am?"

"It doesn't, but I've never been to Maine, and I wanted to know about the wildlife."

"How much will the tow job cost Ma'am?"

"It'll be a total of one hundred- and twenty-dollars."

"Is that the going rate today, Ma'am?"

"Yes," it is. We can't go any cheaper than that.

Chapter 3

Okay, then Ma'am. Oscar heard a gunshot off in the distance.

"Hello? I'm here yet, Ma'am."

"Where did you go?"

"I heard a gunshot, it scared me"

"Was the gunshot close to you?"

"No," it was off in the distance.

That's good to hear.

If it's okay with you, Ma'am, I'm going to hang up with you and wait for the tow truck.

That's okay with me.

“Don't you want to talk to me?”

“Yes,” that is true, Ma’am

Oscar hung up the phone and placed it back in his left pants pocket.

As he was patiently waiting, a truck pulled up beside him; the man honked the horn at Oscar.

This made him curious as to what was going on.

He slowly approached the driver's side of the black truck.

The driver waved for him to come over, he walked over and looked in the car.

“Hello Sir,” what are you doing here?

“I’m a poacher”

“What's your name, friend?”

“My name is Oscar.”

“How long have you been a poacher for?”

“I've been a poacher for one year now”

“Don't you know that's illegal?”

“Yes,” I know, and I don't care, and I'm an alcoholic.

I hope that you aren't drunk while you’re driving right now.

“I have had two beers, and I may have a third.”

“Are you practicing being a policeman?”

“No,” I’m just looking out for you.

“Thank you, but I'm the way I am, and I won't change for anyone.”

“Were you the one that shot the gun?”

“Yes,” and I don't remember why I shot the gun in the first place.

“Would you like to see my gun?”

“Yes,” Sir.

The man took his rifle out of the rifle rack and almost dropped the gun on his lap.

Here you are, Oscar, and he gently gave it to him.

“Do you know the caliber of this gun?”

“No,” I don't know.

Just then, Oscar saw red and blue blinking lights and quickly handed the gun back to the man and hoofed it deep into the woods.

He stood behind a large oak tree and looked around to see what would happen next.

The truck man drove backwards instead of going in front and crashed into the policemen's car.

Oscar walked further towards the police officer to see what he was saying.

He hid behind another tree and kept a watchful eye on the situation.

He saw that the man tried to run but fell flat on his face.

The policeman yelled; don't you make another move.

The policeman wrapped the handcuffs tightly around the man's hands.

The man yelled out; you are hurting me, officer.

The officer said nothing back to the man. I can smell alcohol on your breath.

"How many beers have you had today?"

"Uh, I think I had two, well you better know."

Just then, the man tried to kick the officer.

Nice try, Sir, but you aren't getting away this time.

You’re over the limit with how much alcohol that you have in your truck.

You crashed into the front of my cruiser; I don't appreciate that.

It was an accident, officer, I swear. Just be quiet, you know that you can't drive drunk around here.

No more excuses from you.

Chapter 4

My cruiser's front bumper is barely hanging on, and you broke the right headlight, the hood is bent in.

"You're going to pay for this."

"Your pitiful, you can't even walk in a straight line. Thank you, officer."

"Are you trying to be funny with me?"

"Yes," knock it off.

None of what's happening here is funny.

Sit down in the back seat, I'm going to do the breathalyzer on you.

Then the officer turned on the breathalyzer, it wouldn't read anything.

You're so drunk that you ruined my breathalyzer.

Stop laughing at me, remember you are still going to jail, Sir, for the best part of two years.

You don't know that officer, yes, I do, now be quiet.

The officer pushed the man over further on the back seat and slammed the right rear door shut.

Oscar was shocked at how rough the police officer was with the man.

The officer took out his flashlight and walked over to the guy's truck, and he opened the driver's side door and climbed into the car.

Oscar could see that the officer was rummaging through things in the car.

Five minutes later, the officer climbed back out of the truck and bumped his head on the way out.

Then the officer slammed the driver's side door and rubbed his head.

The officer couldn’t see where Oscar was hiding.

As the officer was walking back to his car, a rabid fox came running out of the woods and ran towards him from his left side.

As soon as he saw the fox, he pulled out his pistol and shot it immediately.

The officer quickly placed his pistol back in the holster and got in his car.

Then he sped off at a high rate of speed.

Oscar thought to himself; these woods are scary.

You don't know what animal will jump out at you? Chills went down his spine.

He eventually was able to shake off the chills; then the cold wind began to blow in.

He developed goosebumps on his arms and legs.

He wasn’t prepared for the cold weather.

So, he ran back to his truck and got into it as fast as he could.

He thought to himself; it's getting colder by the minute out there.

As he was walking through the woods, he saw a man sitting in a folding chair wearing raggedy clothing.

He was wearing a necklace with a glowing gem on it. Since the man didn't see him right away, he must have been sleeping.

When he was about to walk away, the men who woke up and said to him hold on a minute.

I'd like to tell you my story, Oscar sat down on the ground.

I never knew that these woods had a secret, I'm going to take you somewhere.

You'll see the most beautiful things, but you'll have to promise me that you'll stay by my side.

I discovered this place two years ago, and I haven't showed it to anyone.

I find that to be rather peculiar, it's because I don't have any friends.

"Are you homeless?"

"Yes," I am.

They slowly entered the portal; in a minute they were in another world.

"You see those rows of trees over there?"

"Yes," I do.

I'll just walk past them, no you can't or they will come together and crush you.

Wait for a breeze and walk in the zigzag past them, if we're going to cross we need to go now.

Both men walked a zigzag past the trees, to me those trees are just weird.

I'm surprised that someone hasn't cut them down yet, me too.

Suddenly the ground began to move, you can't stand back there for very long, thanks for telling me.

Watch out there's a vine snake in that tree, I doubt that thing could do anything to us anyway.

"Is the sky always orange and blue like that?"

"Yes," it is.

"What's making that chirping sound?"

"It's a dragon bird."

In that lake up ahead of us, lives rainbow snakes.

After exploring the lake and the rest of the places, they saw even more odd creatures.

Several dragon birds flew past them, watch them they'll spit fire.

After a few more hours, they were both tired and went back home through the portal.

www.ingramcontent.com/pod-product-compliance
Lightning Source LLC
LaVergne TN
LVHW040928150826
845672LV00007B/2263

* 9 7 9 8 8 4 7 4 0 9 2 1 6 *